Survival tip 1

Prepare well

As soon as Ben saw the girl he knew she would be a pain.

They were both waiting in line to try out for a new kid's TV show. It was called *Survival Island*.

"Why am I here?" Ben muttered to himself.

The girl heard him.

"To win," she said. "That's the point."

Ben groaned. The girl was one of those kids who wanted to win everything.

He was only there because his mum had seen an advert.

KIDS NEEDED FOR A NEW TV SHOW.

We'll put you in teams and take you to an island.

You must use your survival skills to win.

There will be surprises along the way!

You will need to be ready to go as soon as we choose you.

You will be away from home for ten days.

5

Ben's mum had got all excited.

"You love nature. You could do that," she told him. "Go on, Ben. I'd love to tell everyone that you are on TV."

In the end Ben agreed. He wanted to make his mum happy.

The good news was Ben got chosen for the show. But there was bad news too. The TV people put him in a team with the girl who wanted to win. Her name was Ella.

"What survival skills do you know?" she demanded.

"Er...none really," replied Ben. "I know stuff about animals mostly."

Ella made a face. Ben thought she was about to say something rude, but then one of the TV people stood up.

"The show starts here!" the man said. "The teams will travel to the island by helicopter. Team One. You go first."

He pointed at Ella and Ben.

Survival tip 2

Choose a good camp

A helicopter took Ben and Ella to an island off the coast. They were given backpacks, a wheelbarrow full of firewood and camping stuff.

"I'm going back to get the other teams," said the pilot. "The camera crew will come by boat and bring food supplies. Good luck."

He handed them a sheet of paper.

"If we want to win we have to find the best campsite ever," said Ella.

She rushed off, leaving Ben to push the wheelbarrow.

11

"How about camping there?" Ben pointed.

"Don't be silly," said Ella. "It's at the bottom of a slope. If it rains the water will flow into our tents. We'll lose marks."

Ben felt stupid. He wished that Ella wasn't so keen on winning.

On and on they walked, towards a hill in the middle of the island.

Ben spotted a cliff at the bottom of the hill.
It had a small cave.

"That looks like a good spot," he said. "We
could put the wheelbarrow in the cave."

Ella agreed. "We need to put up our tents right
away," she said.

Then it began to rain.

"We need to shelter in the cave," cried Ben.

But Ella didn't want to go inside.

"It might have bats," she groaned.

"Bats won't hurt you," said Ben, but Ella still
wouldn't go in.

Ella tried her mobile phone.

"There's no signal," she cried. "How could there be no signal?"

"It's OK," said Ben. "Come on inside."

The wind began to howl above their heads.

Survival tip 3

Stay warm

The rain pelted down and the wind began to roar like a monster. In the end Ella *had* to huddle in the cave with Ben.

"I'm really scared of bats," she admitted. "Sorry. What an idiot I am."

"It's alright," Ben told her. "Actually, I don't think there are any bats here."

"How do you know that?" asked Ella.

"Animals are my thing, remember?" Ben replied.

"OK, Animal Boy. I believe you," Ella nodded.

It was starting to get dark. They had to switch on their torches.

"Put on lots of clothing," Ella told Ben. "It'll help you stay warm. And sit on your backpack too. You need to stay off the cold ground."

"How do you know that?" asked Ben.

"Survival stuff is my thing, remember?"
she replied.

Ben was pleased when Ella smiled. It was the
first time he'd seen her do it.

"We should start a camp fire," said Ella.
"But let's eat and drink first. We'll feel better."

They found two snack bars and water bottles in
their backpacks.

Ella was right. Eating and drinking did make
them feel better.

"I don't think I can go to sleep in here," Ella said. "What about you, Animal Boy?"

Ben didn't answer. He was listening.

"What's wrong?" Ella asked. Then she heard a noise too. "There's something outside! What is it?" she cried.

Ben tried to think. What kind of animal could it be? It sounded big.

Suddenly a massive shadow fell on the cave wall. The monster thing was at the entrance!

"Hello," it said.

Survival tip 4

Cope with surprises

A man stumbled into the cave.

"I saw your torchlight," he told them.

Ben shone his torch onto the man's face.

"Wow!" Ella gasped. "You're Adam Mills. I've seen you on TV. You're in *Jungle Days*. That's my favourite TV show!"

"That's right," the man smiled. "I play the dad."

"Sorry," interrupted Ben. "Am I missing something here?"

"You must have seen *Jungle Days*," Ella cried. "It's a show about a family who live in a jungle. They have adventures."

"Oh, right," said Ben, looking blank.

"Each team in this contest gets a celebrity to help them," Adam said. "You got me. I'm your first surprise."

"That's amazing!" cried Ella. "You know all about survival. Now we're going to win, no problem!"

Adam looked embarrassed. He quickly changed the subject.

"I was dropped off this afternoon," he said, "but I still haven't seen the camera crew. Have you? Maybe we should try to ring them."

"We can't ring," Ella explained. "There's no phone signal. I just tried."

"That's a bit rubbish," Adam said. "Is that a snack bar?"

He took the last bar from the top of Ella's pack.

Ella laughed and clapped her hands.

"Adam is great at making camp fires," she told Ben. "He does it lots on *Jungle Days*. There's no room to make one in here now. But we can make one outside in the morning."

"All I want in the morning is a cup of coffee," Adam grinned. "And a chocolate brownie."

Survival tip 5

Build a fire

It was a long cold night in the cave and nobody slept well.

As soon as it got light they crept outside. It was less windy and the rain had stopped.

Ella seemed the happiest. She started to talk about winning again.

"Come on team!" she cried. "Let's build a camp fire. We'll get points for that! We should start with small bits of wood at the bottom. Am I right, Adam?"

Adam just shrugged.

The fire didn't take long to get going. Ella did it all. Ben began to feel glad he was in her team, but he wanted to be useful too.

"Let's climb to the top of the hill," he suggested. "We might spot the camera crew. I'm starving and they are bringing the food!"

"Good idea," Ella agreed. "But someone has to stay here. We need to keep the fire going."

31

"I'll stay," said Adam. "If you bump into the camera crew ask them for coffee, will you?"

Ella and Ben found a rocky path. It led up from the cave to the top of the hill. The view was amazing! They could see waves crashing onto the shore, but there was nobody around.

Then they spotted a dark shape coming up the hill. It waved its arms. It was Adam.

"Did you find the TV people?" he called.
He reached them and sat down on a rock.

"The fire went out," he told them.

"What?" Ella gasped. "How did that happen?
Did you put wood on it?"

"Sorry. Was I supposed to?" Adam replied.

Survival tip 6

Stay positive

Ella was furious. "I thought you knew all about survival," she shouted.

"I'm sorry," Adam sighed. "I'm not really a survival expert. I'm just an actor! I can't cook an egg! I'm only here because I need more work. *Jungle Days* has finished."

Ella glared at him, then stomped off down the hill.

Back at camp they put up the tents and sorted out their things. Nobody said much, and no camera crew turned up. Ben began to wonder if there was a problem. Then his tummy rumbled and Adam heard it.

"We had to pretend to eat ants on *Jungle Days*," Adam said. "They weren't real — just currants. Then a real ant got up my trouser leg!"

He hopped around, doing a funny dance.

Ben laughed and even Ella had to smile. Adam looked pleased.

"I can't make a fire," he said, "but I can make you laugh. I hope that's helpful."

Ben nodded. Laughing had helped. It had taken his mind off his hunger.

It seemed a good idea to take their mind off everything. Ben decided it was his turn. He told the others about the seabirds that lived on the island.

"You're a genius, Animal Boy," Ella grinned.

She set a pan on the fire and boiled some water. Then she pulled out a packet of powder from her backpack and made hot chocolate.

For a moment things didn't seem so bad. They had passed the time, and they all felt they had helped in some way.

But still nobody came.

Work as a team

By nightfall, the crew had still not turned up.

"At least we have tents and a fire now," said Ben.

"But no food!" Ella reminded him. She crawled into her tent. "I'm going to dream of burger and chips," she said. "Good night!"

Ben lay in his tent and listened to the wind. He missed his Mum. He missed his soft bed at home. And he was starving hungry. He had never felt so low.

The next day the three of them went down to the shore.

"It's too windy for a helicopter or boat," said Ella. "We'll be stuck here for a while. Alone."

Their tummies were beginning to ache. Were they going to starve? Things looked pretty bad.

Then Ben had an idea.

"There will be mussels on the rocks when the tide goes out," he said. "We can eat those."

Ella looked down at her feet. "We will have to," she sniffed.

For the first time, tears rolled down Ella's cheeks. Ben felt helpless. He didn't know what to say to make things better. They weren't a brilliant survival team. They were just three unhappy people.

Then Ben looked out to sea and saw something wonderful. "Look!" he cried.

Three dolphins were swimming in the bay. Suddenly they all jumped out of the water together in perfect time.

"See Ella!" said Ben. "We are not alone!"

Ella brushed away a tear.

"You're right!" she smiled. "It's a sign that we can do this. We have to work together, like the dolphins. We have to make a plan."

Adam nodded.

"Let's give this our best shot," he said. "We'll give ourselves a new name – Team Dolphin!"

Survival tip 8

Make a plan

Ben, Ella and Adam went back to camp and made a list of things to do.

They had to find more water, food and dry wood for the fire.

Ben and Ella found a stream and followed it.
Finally, they found the spot where it bubbled
out of the ground.

"The water is cleaner here," said Ella. "We will
still need to boil it, though."

They filled their water bottles and carried them
back to camp.

Adam found some dry sticks and logs on the beach. He carried them back to the camp for the fire.

Being busy made them all feel better. Adam even made up a silly song.

"The Dolphin Team found a stream!" he sang.

In the afternoon they collected mussels from the shore. The tide was out, so they could twist the plump shells off the rocks.

Ben had picked mussels on holiday with his mum, so he knew the rules.

"Only pick shiny ones," he told the others. "They must be closed too. We don't want any with holes. They'll be bad."

When the team got back to camp they scrubbed the mussels. Then they pulled out the tiny strings that dangled from the shells.

Ben popped the mussels in a pan and cooked them over the fire.

"Only eat ones that open," he told the others.

"Yes chef," Adam grinned. "You should be on a cookery show!"

All the mussels opened up perfectly. They tasted of the sea.

That night everyone slept well. They were filled with hot food and tired out. And as they slept, the dolphins in the bay jumped in the moonlight.

Survival tip 9

Stay dry

The next day Team Dolphin woke up to the sound of rain. Adam looked out of his tent.

"That's not good news," he said. "Let's stay in our sleeping bags."

When the rain stopped Adam and Ben came out. Ella didn't.

"I can't stop shivering," she called. "My tent leaked and my sleeping bag got wet."

She sat shaking in her tent. Adam frowned when he saw her.

"You need to put on dry clothes," said Adam. "I'll hang your sleeping bag up to dry."

He gave Ella his own sleeping bag.

"Wrap yourself in this," he told her. "Ben, you get the fire going," he went on. "Ella needs a hot drink."

"You sound like the dad in *Jungle Days*," Ella smiled weakly.

Ben made Ella a hot chocolate. "It's the last one," he told her. "Make the most of it."

Ella cupped her hands round the warm mug. "Yum!" she grinned.

"Do you want mussels for breakfast?" Adam asked. "I'll go and collect some."

He marched off with a pan in his hand.

"Dolphin Team. Lean and mean!" he sang.

"I'm glad Adam is here," smiled Ella. "And you, Ben. Thank you for finding the mussels. I'm glad we saw the dolphins, too. Do you think they spotted us on the beach?"

Ben laughed. "I bet they smelled us," he said. "I need a good wash!"

"We must look a mess," laughed Ella.

"Speak for yourself," Ben replied.

"You look great!" said another voice.

Ella and Ben spun round. A woman was pointing a camera at them. A soundman was recording what they said. It was the TV crew!

Adam stood behind them, grinning like a mad man. He was holding a hot cup of coffee.

Survival tip 10

Enjoy it!

"It's still too windy for helicopters," the camera woman explained. "We finally got here by boat. You were the first team to arrive. Then the gale hit and we had to leave you on your own. But we knew you would be safe with Adam."

Adam stepped forward.

"Actually, these two kids kept *me* safe," he said.
"They should get a medal."

"Can we have a sandwich first?" asked Ben.

The crew took Ben, Ella and Adam back to the mainland by boat.

"The show has been put on hold," said the soundman.

"Then why are you still filming?" asked Ella.

"You're a news story now. You're the kids who got stuck on an island," he replied.

Ben rang his mum as soon as he could.

"I'm on my way to pick you up!" she cried. "You're on TV, by the way. It looks as if you need a bath."

It was very busy for a few days. Everyone wanted to interview Ben and Ella. But soon they were left to get on with life.

Ella started her own survival blog. Adam got a new part on TV. He played a crazy alien dad this time. Ben thought that was a great part for Adam. He was a bit crazy, after all.

As for Ben, he continued to cook delicious mussels. He found they tasted even better with butter, onions and garlic. And every day he patted his warm soft bed to remind himself how cosy and comfy it was.

A few weeks later, Ben was in his room when he heard a shout. Someone was calling him. It was Ella. She was standing outside, waving up at him.

"Hey, Animal Boy!" she yelled. "I had a letter from the TV people. They want us to go on the show again. We have another chance to win. What do you say? Shall we go back to *Survival Island*?"

Ben sat back on his bed. He thought for a moment. Then he smiled and grabbed his bag...